Lourdes

Robert Hugh Benson

Contents

LOURDES

BY

Robert Hugh Benson

PREFACE.

Since writing the following pages six years ago, I have had the privilege of meeting a famous French scientist--to whom we owe one of the greatest discoveries of recent years--who has made a special study of Lourdes and its phenomena, and of hearing him comment upon what takes place there. He is, himself, at present, not a practising Catholic; and this fact lends peculiar interest to his opinions. His conclusions, so far as he has formulated them, are as follows:

(1) That no scientific hypothesis up to the present accounts satisfactorily for the phenomena. Upon his saying this to me I breathed the word "suggestion"; and his answer was to laugh in my face, and to tell me, practically, that this is the most ludicrous hypothesis of all.

(2) That, so far as he can see, the one thing necessary for such cures as he himself has witnessed or verified, is the atmosphere of prayer. Where this rises to intensity the number of cures rises with it; where this sinks, the cures sink too.

(3) That he is inclined to think that there is a transference of vitalizing force either from the energetic faith of the sufferer, or from that of the bystanders. He instanced an example in which his wife, herself a qualified physician, took part. She held in her arms a child, aged two and a half years, blind from birth, during the procession of the Blessed Sacrament. As the monstrance came opposite, tears began to stream from the child's eyes, hitherto closed. When it had passed, the child's eyes were open and seeing. This Mme. ---- tested by dangling her bracelet before the child, who immediately clutched at it, but, from the fact that she had never learned to calculate distance, at first failed to seize it. At the close of the procession Mme. ----, who herself related to me the story, was conscious of an extraordinary exhaustion for which there was no ordinary explanation. I give this suggestion as the scientist gave it to me--the suggestion of some kind of **transference** of vitality; and

make no comment upon it, beyond saying that, superficially at any rate, it does not appear to me to conflict with the various accounts of miracles given in the Gospel in which the faith of the bystanders, as well as of sufferers, appeared to be as integral an element in the miracle as the virtue which worked it.

Owing to the time that has elapsed since the following pages were written for the *Ave Maria*--by the kindness of whose editor they are reprinted now--it is impossible for me to verify the spelling of all the names that occur in the course of the narrative. I made notes while at Lourdes, and from those notes wrote my account; it is therefore extremely probable that small errors of spelling may have crept in, which I am now unable to correct.

ROBERT HUGH BENSON.

I.

The first sign of our approach to Lourdes was a vast wooden cross, crowning a pointed hill. We had been travelling all day, through the August sunlight, humming along the straight French roads beneath the endless avenues; now across a rich plain, with the road banked on either side to avert the spring torrents from the Pyrenees; now again mounting and descending a sudden shoulder of hill. A few minutes ago we had passed into Tarbes, the cathedral city of the diocese in which Lourdes lies; and there, owing to a little accident, we had been obliged to halt, while the wheels of the car were lifted, with incredible ingenuity, from the deep gutter into which the chauffeur had, with the best intentions, steered them. It was here, in the black eyes, the dominant profiles, the bright colours, the absorbed childish interest of the crowd, in their comments, their laughter, their seriousness, and their accent, that the South showed itself almost unmixed. It was market-day in Tarbes; and when once more we were on our way, we still went slowly; passing, almost all the way into Lourdes itself, a long-drawn procession--carts and foot passengers, oxen, horses, dogs, and children--drawing nearer every minute toward that ring of solemn blue hills that barred the view to Spain.

It is difficult to describe with what sensations I came to Lourdes. As a Christian man, I did not dare to deny that miracles happened; as a reasonably humble man, I did not dare to deny that they happened at Lourdes; yet, I suppose, my attitude even up to now had been that of a reverent agnostic--the attitude, in fact, of a majority of Christians on this particular point--Christians, that is, who resemble the Apostle Thomas in his less agreeable aspect. I had heard and read a good deal about psychology, about the effect of mind on matter and of nerves on tissue; I had reflected upon the infection of an ardent crowd; I had read Zola's dishonest book;[1] and these things, coupled with the extreme difficulty which the imagination finds in realizing what it has never experienced--since, after all, miracles are confessedly miraculous, and therefore unusual--the effect of all this was to render my mental state a singularly detached one. I believed? Yes, I suppose so; but it was a halting act of faith pure and simple; it was not yet either sight or real conviction.

The cross, then, was the first glimpse of Lourdes' presence; and ten minutes later we were in the town itself.

Lourdes is not beautiful, though it must once have been. It was once a little Franco-Spanish town, set in the lap of the hills, with a swift, broad, shallow stream, the Gave, flowing beneath it. It is now cosmopolitan, and therefore undistinguished. As we passed slowly through the crowded streets--for the National Pilgrimage was but now arriving--we saw endless rows of shops and booths sheltering beneath tall white blank houses, as correct and as expressionless as a brainless, well-bred man. Here and there we passed a great hotel. The crowd about our wheels was almost as cosmopolitan as a Roman crowd. It was largely French, as that is largely Italian; but the Spaniards were there, vivid-faced men and women, severe Britons, solemn Teutons; and, I have no doubt, Italians, Belgians, Flemish and Austrians as well. At least I heard during my three days' stay all the languages that I could recognize, and many that I could not. There were many motor-cars there besides our own, carriages, carts, bell-clanging trams, and the litters of the sick. Presently we dismounted in

1   The epithet is deliberate. He relates in his book, "Lourdes," the story of an imaginary case of a girl, suffering from tuberculosis, who goes to Lourdes as a pilgrim, and is, apparently, cured of her disease. It breaks out, however, again during her return home; and the case would appear therefore to be one of those in which, owing to fierce excitement and the mere power of suggestion, there is a temporary amelioration, but no permanent, or supernatural, cure. Will it be believed that the details of this story, all of which are related with great particularity, and observed by Zola himself, were taken from an actual case that occurred during one of his visits--all the details except the relapse? There was no relapse: the cure was complete and permanent. When Dr. Boissarie later questioned the author as to the honesty of this literary device, saying that he had understood him to have stated that he had come to Lourdes for the purpose of an impartial investigation, Zola answered that the characters in the book were his own, and that he could make them do what he liked. It is on these principles that the book is constructed. It must be added that Zola followed up the case, and had communications with the miraculÉe long after her cure had been shown to be permanent, and before his book appeared.

a side street, and set out to walk to the Grotto, through the hot evening sunshine.

The first sign of sanctity that we saw, as we came out at the end of a street, was the mass of churches built on the rising ground above the river. Imagine first a great oval of open ground, perhaps two hundred by three hundred yards in area, crowded now with groups as busy as ants, partly embraced by two long white curving arms of masonry rising steadily to their junction; at the point on this side where the ends should meet if they were prolonged, stands a white stone image of Our Lady upon a pedestal, crowned, and half surrounded from beneath by some kind of metallic garland arching upward. At the farther end the two curves of masonry of which I have spoken, rising all the way by steps, meet upon a terrace. This terrace is, so to speak, the centre of gravity of the whole.

For just above it stands the flattened dome of the Rosary Church, of which the doors are beneath the terrace, placed upon broad flights of steps. Immediately above the dome is the entrance to the crypt of the basilica; and, above that again, reached by further flights of steps, are the doors of the basilica; and, above it, the roof of the church itself, with its soaring white spire high over all.

Let me be frank. These buildings are not really beautiful. They are enormous, but they are not impressive; they are elaborate and fine and white, but they are not graceful. I am not sure what is the matter with them; but I think it is that they appear to be turned out of a machine. They are too trim; they are like a well-dressed man who is not quite a gentleman; they are like a wedding guest; they are *haute-bourgeoise*, they are not the nobility. It is a terrible pity, but I suppose it could not be helped, since they were allowed so little time to grow. There is no sense of reflectiveness about them, no patient growth of character, as in those glorious cathedrals, Amiens, Chartres, Beauvais, which I had so lately seen. There is nothing in reserve; they say everything, they suggest nothing. They have no imaginative vista.

We said not one word to one another. We threaded our way across the ground, diagonally, seeing as we went the Bureau de Constatations (or the office where the doctors sit), contrived near the left arm of the terraced steps; and passed out under the archway, to find ourselves with the churches on our left, and on our right the flowing Gave, confined on this side by a terraced walk, with broad fields beyond the stream.

The first thing I noticed were the three roofs of the *piscines*, on the left side of the road, built under the cliff on which the churches stand. I shall have more to say of them presently, but now it is enough to remark that they resemble three little chapels, joined in one, each with its own doorway; an open paved space lies across the entrances, where the doctors and the priests attend upon the sick. This open space is fenced in all about, to keep out the crowd that perpetually seethes there. We went a few steps farther, worked our way in among the people, and fell on our knees.

Overhead, the cliff towered up, bare hanging rock beneath, grass and soaring trees above; and at the foot of the cliff a tall, irregular cave. There are two openings of this cave; the one, the larger, is like a cage of railings, with the gleam of an altar in the gloom beyond, a hundred burning candles, and sheaves and stacks of crutches clinging to the broken roofs of rock; the other, and smaller, and that farther from us, is an opening in the cliff, shaped somewhat like a ***vesica***. The grass still grows there, with ferns and the famous climbing shrub; and within the entrance, framed in it, stands Mary, in white and blue, as she stood fifty years ago, raised perhaps twenty feet above the ground.

Ah, that image!... I said, "As she stood there!" Yet it could not have been so; for surely even simple Bernadette would not have fallen on her knees. It is too white, it is too blue; it is, like the three churches, placed magnificently, yet not impressive; fine and slender, yet not graceful.

But we knelt there without unreality, with the river running swift behind us; for we knelt where a holy child had once knelt before a radiant vision, and with even more reason; for even if the one, as some say, had been an hallucination, were those sick folk an hallucination? Was Pierre de Rudder's mended leg an hallucination, or the healed wounds of Marie Borel? Or were those hundreds upon hundreds of disused crutches an illusion? Did subjectivity create all these? If so, what greater miracle can be demanded?

And there was more than that. For when later, at ArgelÈs, I looked over the day, I was able to formulate for the first time the extraordinary impressions that Lourdes had given me. There was everything hostile to my peace--an incalculable crowd, an oppressive heat, dust, noise, weariness; there was the disappointment of the churches and the image; there was the sour unfamiliarity of the place and the experience; and yet I was neither troubled nor depressed nor irritated nor disappointed. It appeared to me as if some great benign influence were abroad, soothing and satisfying; lying like a great summer air over all, to quiet and to stimulate. I cannot describe this further; I can only say that it never really left me during those three days, I saw sights that would have saddened me elsewhere--apparent injustices, certain disappointments, dashed hopes that would almost have broken my heart; and yet that great Power was over all, to reconcile, to quiet and to reassure. To leave Lourdes at the end was like leaving home.

After a few minutes before the Grotto, we climbed the hill behind, made an appointment for my Mass on the morrow; and, taking the car again, moved slowly through the crowded streets, and swiftly along the country roads, up to ArgelÈs, nearly a dozen miles away.

II.

We were in Lourdes again next morning a little after six o'clock; and already it might have been high noon, for the streets were one moving mass of pilgrims. From every corner came gusts of singing; and here and there through the crowd already moved the ***brancardiers***--men of every nation with shoulder-straps and cross--bearing the litters with their piteous burdens.

I was to say Mass in the crypt; and when I arrived there at last, the church was full from end to end. The interior was not so disappointing as I had feared. It had a certain solid catacombic gloom beneath its low curved roof, which, if it had not been for the colours and some of the details, might very nearly have come from the hand of a good architect. The arrangements for the pilgrims were as bad as possible; there was no order, no marshalling; they moved crowd against crowd like herds of bewildered sheep. Some were for Communion, some for Mass only, some for confession; and they pushed patiently this way and that in every direction. It was a struggle before I got my vestments; I produced a letter from the Bishop of Rodez, with whom I had lunched a few days before; I argued, I deprecated, I persuaded, I quoted. Everything once more was against my peace of mind; yet I have seldom said Mass with more consolations than in that tiny sanctuary of the high Altar.... An ecclesiastic served, and an old priest knelt devoutly at a prie-Dieu.

When the time for Communion came, I turned about and saw but one sea of faces stretching from the altar rail into as much of the darkness as I could discern. For a quarter of an hour I gave Communion rapidly; then, as soon as another priest could force his way through the crowd, I continued Mass; he had not nearly finished giving Communion when I had ended my thanksgiving. This, too, was the same everywhere--in the crypt, in the basilica, in the Rosary Church, and above all in the Grotto. The average number of Communions every day throughout the year in Lourdes is, I am told, four thousand. In that year of Jubilee, however, Dr. Boissarie informed me, in round numbers, one million Communions were made, sixty thousand Masses were said, with two thousand Communions at each midnight Mass.... Does Jesus Christ go out when Mary comes in? We are told so by non-Catholics. Rather, it seems as if, like the Wise Men of old, men still find the Child with Mary His Mother.

At the close of my Mass, the old priest rose from his place and began to prepare the vessels and arrange the Missal. As soon as I took off the vestments he put them on. I assented passively, supposing him to be the next on the list; I even answered his *Kyrie*. But at the Collect a frantic sacristan burst through the crowd; and from remarks made to the devout old priest and myself, I learned that the next on the list was still waiting in the sacristy, and that this old man was an adroit though pious interloper who had determined not to take "No" for an answer. He finished his Mass. I forbear from comment.

For a while afterward we stood on the terrace above the *piscines*; and, indeed, after breakfast I returned here again alone, and remained during all the morning. It was an extraordinary sight. From the terrace, the cliff fell straight away down to the roofs of the three chapel-like buildings, fifty or sixty feet beneath. Beyond that I could see the paved space, sprinkled with a few moving figures; and, beyond the barrier, the crowd stretching across the roadway and far on either side. Behind them was the clean river and the green meadows, all delicious in the early sunlight.

During that morning I must have seen many hundreds of the sick carried into the baths; for there were almost two thousand sick in Lourdes on that day. I could even watch their faces, white and drawn with pain, or horribly scarred, as they lay directly beneath me, "waiting for some man to put them into the water." I saw men and women of all nations and all ranks attending upon them, carrying them tenderly, fanning their faces, wiping their lips, giving them to drink of the Grotto water. A murmur of thousands of footsteps came up from beneath (this National Pilgrimage of France numbered between eighty and an hundred thousand persons); and loud above the footsteps came the cries of the priests, as they stood in a long row facing the people, with arms extended in the form of a cross. Now and again came a far-off roar of singing from the Grotto to my left, where Masses were said continuously by bishops and favoured priests; or from my right, from the great oval space beneath the steps; and then, on a sudden a great chorus of sound from beneath, as the ***Gloria Patri*** burst out when the end of some decade was reached. All about us was the wheeling earth, the Pyrenees behind, the meadows in front; and over us heaven, with Mary looking down.

Once from beneath during that long morning I heard terrible shrieks, as of a demoniac, that died into moans and ceased. And once I saw a little procession go past from the Grotto, with the Blessed Sacrament in the midst. There was no sensation, no singing. The Lord of all went simply by on some errand of mercy, and men fell on their knees and crossed themselves as He went.

After dÉjeÃ»ner at the Hotel Moderne, where now it was decided that we should stay until the Monday, we went down to the Bureau. At first there were difficulties made, as the doctors were not come; and I occupied a little while in watching the litters unloaded from the wagonettes that brought them gently down to within a hundred yards of the Grotto. Once indeed I was happy to be able to fit a ***brancardier's*** straps into the poles that supported a sick woman. It was all most terrible and most beautiful. Figure after figure was passed along the seats--living crucifixes of pain--and lowered tenderly to the ground, to lie there a moment or two, with the body horribly flat and, as it seemed, almost non-existent beneath the coverlet; and the white face with blazing eyes of anguish, or passive and half dead, to show alone that a human creature lay there. Then one by one each was lifted and swung gently down to the gate of the ***piscines***.

At about three o'clock, after an hour's waiting, I succeeded in getting a certain card passed through the window, and immediately a message came out from Dr. Cox that I was to be admitted. I passed through a barrier, through a couple of rooms, and found myself in the Holy Place of Science, as the Grotto is the Holy Place of Grace.

It is a little room in which perhaps twenty persons can stand with comfort. Again and again I saw more than sixty there. Down one side runs a table, at one end of which sits Dr. Cox; in the centre, facing the room, is the presiding doctor's chair, where, as a rule, Dr. Boissarie is to be found. Dr. Cox set me between him and the president, and I began to observe.

At the farther end of the room is a long glazed case of photographs hung against the wall. Here are photographs of many of the most famous patients. The wounds of Marie Borel are shown there; Marie Borel herself had been present in the Bureau that morning to report upon her excellent health. (She was cured last year instantaneously, in the *piscine*, of a number of running wounds, so deep that they penetrated the intestines.) On the table lay some curious brass objects, which I learned later were models of the bones of Pierre de Rudder's legs. (This man had for eight years suffered from a broken leg and two running wounds--one at the fracture, the other on the foot. These were gangrenous. The ends of the broken bones were seen immediately before the cure, which took place instantaneously at the shrine of Our Lady of Lourdes at Oostacker. Pierre lived rather over twenty years after his sudden and complete restoration to health). For the rest, the room is simple enough. There are a few chairs. Another door leads into a little compartment where the sick can be examined privately; a third and a fourth lead into the open air on either side. There are two windows, looking out respectively on this side and that.

Now I spent a great deal of my time in the Bureau. (I was given presently a "doctor's cross" to wear--consisting of a kind of cardboard with a white upright and red cross-bar--so that I could pass in and out as I wished). I may as well, then, sum up once and for all the impressions I received from observing the methods of the doctors. There were all kinds of doctors there continually--Catholics and free-thinkers, old, young, middle-aged. The cases were discussed with the utmost freedom. Any could ask questions of the miraculÉs or of the other doctors. The certificates of the sick were read aloud. I may observe, too, that if there was any doubt as to the certificates, if there was any question of a merely nervous malady, any conceivable possibility of a mistake, the case was dismissed abruptly. These certificates, then, given by the doctor attending the sick person, dated and signed, are of the utmost importance; for without them no cure is registered. Yet, in spite of these demands, I saw again and again sixty or seventy men, dead silent, staring, listening with all their ears, while some poor uneducated man or woman, smiling radiantly, gave a little history or answered the abrupt kindly questions of the presiding doctor.

Again, and again, too, it seemed to me that all this had been enacted before. There was once upon a time a man born blind who received his sight, and round him there gathered keen-eyed doctors of another kind. They tried to pose him with questions. It was unheard of, they cried, that a man born blind should receive his sight; at least it could not have been as he said. Yet there stood the man in the midst, seeing them as they saw him, and giving his witness. "This," he said, "was the way it was done. Such and such is the name of the Man who cured me. And look for yourselves! I was blind; now I see."

After I had looked and made notes and asked questions of Dr. Cox, Dr. Boissarie came in. I was made known to him; and presently he took me aside, with a Scottish priest (who all through my stay showed me great kindness), and began to ask me questions. It seemed that, since there was no physical miraculÉ present just now, a spiritual miraculÉ would do as well; for he asked me a hundred questions as to my conversion and its causes, and what part prayer played in it; and the doctors crowded round and listened to my halting French.

"It was the need of a divine Leader--an authority--then, that brought you in?"

"Yes, it was that; it was the position of St. Peter in the Scriptures and in history; it was the supernatural unity of the Church. It is impossible to say exactly which argument predominated."

"It was, in fact, the grace of God," smiled the Doctor.

Dr. Boissarie, as also Dr. Cox, was extremely good to me. He is an oldish man, with a keen, clever, wrinkled face; he is of middle-size, and walks very slowly and deliberately; he is a fervent Catholic. He is very sharp and businesslike, but there is an air of wonderful goodness and kindness about him; he takes one by the arm in a very pleasant manner; I have seen dilatory, rambling patients called to their senses in an instant, yet never frightened.

Dr. Cox, who has been at Lourdes for fourteen years, is a typical Englishman, ruddy, with a white moustache. His part is mostly secretarial, it seems; though he too asks questions now and again. It was he who gave me the "doctor's cross," and who later obtained for me an even more exceptional favour, of which I shall speak in the proper place. I heard a tale that he himself had been cured of some illness at Lourdes, but I cannot vouch for it as true. I did not like to ask him outright.

Presently from outside came the sound of organized singing, and the room began to empty. The afternoon procession was coming. I ran to the window that looks toward the Grotto; and there, sitting by an Assumptionist Father--one of that Order who once had, officially, charge of the Grotto, and now unofficially assists at it--I saw the procession go past.

I have no idea of its numbers. I saw only beyond the single line of heads outside the window, an interminable double stream of men go past, each bearing a burning taper and singing as he came. There were persons of every kind in that stream--groups of boys and young men, with their priest beating time in the midst; middle-aged men and old men. I saw again and again that kind of face which a foolish Briton is accustomed to regard as absurd--a military, musketeer profile, immense moustaches and imperial, and hair ***en brosse***. Yet indeed there was nothing absurd. It was terribly moving, and a lump rose in my throat, as I watched such a sanguine bristling face as one of these, all alight with passion and adoration. Such a man might be a grocer, or a local mayor, or a duke; it was all one; he was a child of Mary; and he loved her with all his heart, and Gabriel's salute was on his lips. Then the priests began to come; long lines of them in black; then white cottas; then gleams of purple; then a pectoral cross or two; and last the great canopy swaying with all its bells and tassels.

III.

Now, it is at the close of the afternoon procession that the sick more usually are healed. I crossed the Bureau to the other window that looks on to what I will call the square, and began to watch for the reappearance of the procession on that side. In front of me was a dense crowd of heads, growing more dense every step up to the barriers that enclose the open space in the midst. It was beyond those barriers, as I knew, that the sick were laid ready for the passing by of Jesus of Nazareth. On the right rose the wide sweep of steps and terraces leading up to the basilica, and every line of stone was crowned with heads. Even on the cliffs beyond, I could see figures coming and going and watching. In all, about eighty thousand persons were present.

Presently the singing grew loud again; the procession had turned the corner and entered the square; and I could see the canopy moving quickly down the middle toward the Rosary Church, for its work was done. The Blessed Sacrament was now to be carried round the lines of the sick, beneath an *ombrellino*.

I shall describe all this later, and more in detail; it is enough just now to say that the Blessed Sacrament went round, that It was carried at last to the steps of the Rosary Church, and that, after the singing of the *Tantum Ergo* by that enormous crowd, Benediction was given. Then the Bureau began to fill, and I turned round for the scientific aspect of the affair.

The first thing that I saw was a little girl, seeming eight or nine years old, who walked in and stood at the other side of the table, to be examined. Her name was Marguerite Vandenabeele--so I read on the certificate--and she had suffered since birth from infantile paralysis, with such a result that she was unable to put her heels to the ground. That morning in the *piscine* she had found herself able to walk properly though her heels were tender from disuse. We looked at her--the doctors who had begun again to fill the room, and myself, with three or four more amateurs. There she stood, very quiet and unexcited, with a slightly flushed face. Some elder person in charge of her gave in the certificate and answered the questions. Then she went away.[2]

Now, I must premise that the cures that took place while I was at Lourdes that August cannot yet be regarded as finally established, since not sufficient time has elapsed for their test and verification.[3] Occasionally there is a relapse soon after the apparent cure, in the case of certain diseases that may be more or less affected by a nervous condition; occasionally claimants are found not to be cured at all. For scientific certainty, therefore, it is better to rely upon cures that have taken place a year, or at least some months previously, in which the restored health is preserved. There are, of course a large number of such cases; I shall come to them presently.[4]

The next patient to enter the room was one Mlle. Bardou. I learned later from her lips that she was a secularized Carmelite nun, expelled from her convent by the French Government. There was the further pathos in her case in the fact that her cure, when I left Lourdes, was believed to be at least doubtful. But now she took her seat, with a radiantly happy face, to hand in her certificate and answer the questions. She had suffered from renal tuberculosis; her certificate proved that. She was here herself, without pain or discomfort, to prove that she no longer suffered. Relief had come during the procession. A question or two was put to her; an arrangement was made for her return after examination; and she went out.

The room was rapidly filling now; there were forty or fifty persons present.

2 *La Voix de Lourdes*, a semi-official paper, gives the following account of her, in its issue of the 23rd: "... Marguerite Vandenabeele, 10 ans, de Nieurlet, hameau de Hedezeele, (Nord), est arrivÉe avec un des trains de Paris, portant un certificat du Docteur Dantois, datÉ de St. Momeleu (Nord) le 25 mai, 1908, la dÉclarant atteinte *d'atrophie de la jambe gauche* avec pied-bot Équin. Elle ne marchait que trÈs difficilement et trÈs pÉniblement. A la sortie de la piscine, vendredi soir, elle a pu marcher facilement. AmenÉe au Bureau MÉdical, on l'a dÉbarrassÉe de l'appareil dans lequel Était enfermÉ son pied. Depuis, elle marche bien, et parait guÉrie."

3 This was written in the autumn of the year 1908, in which this visit of mine took place.

4 Since 1888 the registered cures are estimated as follows: '88, 57; '89, 44; '90, 80; '91, 53; '92, 99; '93, 91; '94, 127; '95, 163; '96, 145; '97, 163; '98, 243; '99, 174; 1900, 160; '01, 171; '02, 164; '03, 161; '04, 140; '05, 157; '06, 148; '07, 109.

There was a sudden stir; those who sat rose up; and there came into the room three bishops in purple--from St. Paul in Brazil, the Bishop of Beauvais, and the famous orator, Monseigneur Touchet, of OrlÉans--all of whom had taken part in the procession. These sat down, and the examination went on.

The next to enter was Juliette Gosset, aged twenty-five, from Paris. She had a darkish plain face, and was of middle size. She answered the questions quietly enough, though there was evident a suppressed excitement beneath. She had been cured during the procession, she said; she had stood up and walked. And her illness? She showed a certificate, dated in the previous March, asserting that she suffered gravely from tuberculosis, especially in the right lung; she added herself that hip disease had developed since that time, that one leg had become seven centimetres shorter than the other, and that she had been for some months unable to sit or kneel. Yet here she walked and sat without the smallest apparent discomfort. When she had finished her tale, a doctor pointed out that the certificate said nothing of any hip disease. She assented, explaining again the reason; but added that the hospital where she lodged in Lourdes would corroborate what she said. Then she disappeared into the little private room to be examined.

There followed a nun, pale and black-eyed, who made gestures as she stood by Dr. Boissarie and told her story. She spoke very rapidly. I learned that she had been suffering from a severe internal malady, and that she had been cured instantaneously in the *piscine*. She handed in her certificate, and then she, too, vanished.

After a few minutes there returned the doctor who had examined Juliette Gosset. Now, I think it should impress the incredulous that this case was pronounced unsatisfactory, and will not, probably, appear upon the registers. It was perfectly true that the girl had had tuberculosis, and that now nothing was to be detected except the very faintest symptom--so faint as to be negligible--in the right lung. It appeared to be true also that she had had hip disease, since there were upon her body certain marks of treatment by burning; and that her legs were now of an exactly equal length. But, firstly, the certificate was five months old, secondly, it made no mention of hip disease; thirdly, seven centimetres was almost too large a measure to be believed. The case then was referred back for further investigation; and there it stood when I left Lourdes. The doctors shook their heads considerably over the seven centimetres.

There followed next one of the most curious instances of all. It was an old miraculÉe who came back to report; her case is reported at length in Dr. Boissarie's Å'uvre de Lourdes, on pages 299-308.[5] Her name was Marie Cools, and she came from Anvers, suffering apparently from ***mal de Pott***, and paralysis and anÃ¦sthesia of the legs. This state had lasted for about three years. The doctors consulted differed as to her case: two diagnosing it as mentioned above, two as hysteria. For ten months she had suffered, moreover, from constant feverishness; she was continually sick, and the work of digestion was painful and difficult. There was a marked lateral deviation of the spinal column, with atrophy of the leg muscles. At the second bath she began to improve, and the pains in the back ceased; at the fourth bath the paralysis vanished, her appetite came steadily back, and the sickness ceased. Now she came in to announce her continued good health.

There are a number of interesting facts as to this case; and the first is the witness of the infidel doctor who sent her to Lourdes, since it seemed to him that "religious suggestion," was the only hope left. He, by the way, had diagnosed her case as one of hysteria. "It had a result," he writes, "which I, though an unbeliever, can characterize only as marvellous. Marie Cools returned completely, absolutely cured. No trace of paralysis or anÃ¦sthesia. She is actually on her feet; and, two hospital servants having been stricken by typhoid, she is taking the place of one of them." Another interesting fact is that a positive storm raged at Anvers over her cure, and that Dr. Van de Vorst was at the ensuing election dismissed from the hospital, with at least a suspicion that the cause of his dismissal lay in his having advised the girl to go to Lourdes at all.

Dr. Boissarie makes an interesting comment or two on the case, allowing that it may perhaps have been hysteria, though this is not at all certain. "When we have to do with nervous maladies, we must always remember the rules of Benedict XIV.: 'The miracle cannot consist in the cessation of the crises, but in the cessation of the nervous state which produces them.'" It is this that has been accomplished in the case of Marie Cools. And again: "Either Marie Cools is not cured, or there is in her cure something other than suggestion, even religious. It is high time to leave that tale alone, and to cease to class under the title of religious suggestion two orders

---

5   My notes are rather illegible at this point, but I make no doubt that this was Marie Cools.

of facts completely distinct--superficial and momentary modifications, and consti-
tutional modifications so profound that science cannot explain them. I repeat: to
make of an hysterical patient one whose equilibrium is perfect ... is a thing more
difficult than the cure of a wound."

So he wrote at the time of her apparent cure, hesitating still as to its perma-
nence. And here, before my eyes and his, she stood again, healthy and well.

And so at last I went back to dinner. A very different scene followed. For a
couple of hours we had been materialists, concerning ourselves not with what Mary
had done by grace--at least not in that aspect--but with what nature showed to have
been done, by whatever agency, in itself. Now once more we turned to Mary.

It was dark when we arrived at the square, but the whole place was alive with
earthly lights. High up to our left hung the church, outlined in fire--tawdry, I dare
say, with its fairy lights of electricity, yet speaking to three-quarters of this crowd in
the highest language they knew. Light, after all, is the most heavenly thing we pos-
sess. Does it matter so very much if it is decked out and arranged in what to superior
persons appears a finikin fashion?

The crowd itself had become a serpent of fire, writhing here below in endlessly
intricate coils; up there along the steps and parapets, a long-drawn, slow-moving
line; and from the whole incalculable number came gusts and roars of singing, for
each carried a burning torch and sang with his group. The music was of all kinds.
Now and again came the **Laudate Mariam** from one company, following to some
degree the general movement of the procession, and singing from little paper-books
which each read by the light of his wind-blown lantern; now the **Gloria Patri**, as
a band came past reciting the Rosary; but above all pealed the ballad of Bernadette,
describing how the little child went one day by the banks of the Gave, how she
heard the thunderous sound, and, turning, saw the Lady, with all the rest of the
sweet story, each stanza ending with that

    Ave, Ave, Ave Maria!

that I think will ring in my ears till I die.

It was an astounding sight to see that crowd and to hear that singing, and to
watch each group as it came past--now girls, now boys, now stalwart young men,
now old veteran pilgrims, now a bent old woman; each face illumined by the soft
paper-shrouded candle, and each mouth singing to Mary. Hardly one in a thousand

of those came to be cured of any sickness; perhaps not one in five hundred had any friend among the patients; yet here they were, drawn across miles of hot France, to give, not to get. Can France, then, be so rotten?

As I dropped off to sleep that night, the last sound of which I was conscious was, still that cannon-like chorus, coming from the direction of the square:

Ave, Ave, Ave Maria!
Ave, Ave, Ave Maria!

IV.

I awoke to that singing again, in my room above the door of the hotel; and went down presently to say my Mass in the Rosary Church, where, by the kindness of the Scottish priest of whom I have spoken, an altar had been reserved for me. The Rosary Church is tolerably fine within. It has an immense flattened dome, beyond which stands the high altar; and round about are fifteen chapels dedicated to the Fifteen Mysteries, which are painted above their respective altars.

But I was to say Mass in a little temporary chapel to the left of the entrance, formed, I suppose, out of what usually serves as some kind of a sacristy. The place was hardly forty feet long; its high altar, at which I both vested and said Mass, was at the farther end; but each side, too, was occupied by three priests, celebrating simultaneously upon altar-stones laid on long, continuous boards that ran the length of the chapel. The whole of the rest of the space was crammed to overflowing; indeed it had been scarcely possible to get entrance to the chapel at all, so vast was the crowd in the great church outside.

After breakfast I went down to the Bureau once more, and found business already begun. The first case, which was proceeding as I entered, was that of a woman (whose name I could not catch) who had been cured of consumption in the previous year, and who now came back to report a state of continued good health. Her brother-in-law came with her, and she remarked with pleasure that the whole family was now returning to the practice of religion. During this investigation I noticed also Juliette Gosset seated at the table, apparently in robust health.

There followed Natalie Audivin, a young woman who declared that she had been cured in the previous year, and that she supposed her case had been entered in the books; but at the moment, at any rate, her name could not be found, and for the present the case was dismissed.

I now saw a Capuchin priest in the room--a small, rosy, bearded man--and supposed that he was present merely as a spectator; but a minute or two later Dr. Boissarie caught sight of him, and presently was showing him off to me, much to his smiling embarrassment. He had caught consumption of the intestines, it seemed, some years before, from attending upon two of his dying brethren, and had come to Lourdes almost at his last gasp in the year 1900 A. D. Here he stood, smiling and rosy.

There followed Mademoiselle Madeleine Laure, cured of severe internal troubles (I did not catch the details) in the previous year.

Presently the Bishop of Dalmatia came in, and sat in his chair opposite me, while we heard the account of Miss Noemie Nightingale, of Upper Norwood, cured in the previous June of deafness, rising, in the case of one ear at least, from a perforation of the drum. She was present at the ***piscines***, when on a sudden she had felt excruciating pains in the ears. The next she knew was that she heard the ***Magnificat*** being sung in honour of her cure.

Mademoiselle Marie Bardou came in about this time, and passed through to the inner room to be examined; while we received from a doctor a report of the lame child whom we had seen on the previous day. All was as had been said. She could now put her heels to the ground and walk. It seemed she had been conscious of a sensation of hammering in her feet at the moment of the cure, followed by a feeling of relief.

And so they went on. Next came Mademoiselle EugÉnie Meunier, cured two months before of fistula. She had given her certificate into the care of her curÉ, who could not at this moment be found--naturally enough, as she had made no appointment with him!--but she was allowed to tell her story, and to show a copy of her parish magazine in which her story was given. She had had in her body one wound of ten centimetres in size. After bathing one evening she had experienced relief; by the next morning the wound, which had flowed for six months, was completely closed, and had remained so. Her strength and appetite had returned. This cure had taken place in her own lodging, since her state was such that she was forbidden to go to the Grotto.

The next case was that of a woman with paralysis, who was entered provisionally as one of the "ameliorations." She was now able to walk, but the use of her hand was not yet fully restored. She was sent back to the *piscines*, and ordered to report again later.

The next was a boy of about twelve years old, Hilaire Ferraud, cured of a terrible disease of the bone three years before. Until that time he was unable to walk without support. He had been cured in the *piscines*. He had been well ever since. He followed the trade of a carpenter. And now he hopped solemnly, first on one leg and then on the other, to the door and back, to show his complete recovery. Further, he had had running wounds on one leg, now healed. His statements were verified.

The next was an oldish man, who came accompanied by his tall, black-bearded son, to report on his continued good health since his recovery, eight years previously, from neurasthenia and insanity. He had had the illusion of being persecuted, with suicidal tendencies; he had been told he could not travel twenty miles, and he had travelled over eight hundred kilometres, after four years' isolation. He had stayed a few months in Lourdes, bathing in the *piscines*, and the obsession had left him. His statements were verified; he was congratulated and dismissed.

There followed Emma Mourat to report; and then Madame Simonet, cured eight years ago of a cystic tumour in the abdomen. She had been sitting in one of the churches, I think, when there was a sudden discharge of matter, and a sense of relief. On the morrow, after another bath, the sense of discomfort had finally disappeared. During Madame Simonet's examination, as the crowd was great, several persons were dismissed till a later hour.

There followed another old patient to report. She had been cured two years before of myelitis and an enormous tumour that, after twenty-two years of suffering, had been declared "incurable" in her certificate. The cure had taken place during the procession, in the course of which she suddenly felt herself, she said, impelled to rise from her litter. Her appetite had returned and she had enjoyed admirable health ever since. Her name was looked up, and the details verified.

There followed Madame FranÃ§ois and some doctor's evidence. Nine years ago she had been cured of fistula in the arm. She had been operated upon five times; finally, as her arm measured a circumference of seventy-two centimetres, amputation had been declared necessary. She had refused, and had come to Lourdes. Her cure occupied three days, at the end of which her arm had resumed its normal size of twenty-five centimetres. She showed her arm, with faint scars visible upon it; it was again measured and found normal.

It was an amazing morning. Here I had sat for nearly three hours, seeing with my own eyes persons of all ages and both sexes, suffering from every variety of disease, present themselves before sixty or seventy doctors, saying that they had been cured miraculously by the Mother of God. Various periods had elapsed since their cures--a day, two or three months, one year, eight years, nine years. These persons had been operated upon, treated, subjected to agonizing remedies; one or two had been declared actually incurable; and then, either in an instant, or during the lapse of two or three days, or two or three months, had been restored to health by prayer and the application of a little water in no way remarkable for physical qualities.

What do the doctors say to this? Some confess frankly that it is miraculous in the literal sense of the term, and join with the patients in praising Mary and her Divine Son. Some say nothing; some are content to say that science at its present stage cannot account for it all, but that in a few years, no doubt ... and the rest of it. I did not hear any say that: "He casteth out devils by Beelzebub, the prince of devils"; but that is accounted for by the fact that those who might wish to say it do not believe in Beelzebub.

But will science ever account for it all? That I leave to God. All that I can say is that, if so, it is surely as wonderful as any miracle, that the Church should have hit upon a secret that the scientists have missed. But is there not a simpler way of accounting for it? For read and consider the human evidence as regards Bernadette--her age, her simplicity, her appearance of ecstasy. She said that she saw this Lady eighteen times; on one of these occasions, in the presence of bystanders. She was bidden, she said, to go to the water. She turned to go down to the Gave, but was recalled and bidden to dig in the earth of the Grotto. She did so, and a little muddy water appeared where no soul in the village knew that there was water. Hour by hour this water waxed in volume; to-day it pours out in an endless stream, is conducted through the *piscines*; and it is after washing in this water that bodies are healed in a fashion for which "science cannot account." Perhaps it cannot. Perhaps it is not intended. But there are things besides science, and one of them is religion. Is not the evidence tolerably strong? Or is it a series of coincidences that the child had an hallucination, devised some trick with the water, and that this water happens to be an occasion of healing people declared incurable by known means?

What is the good of these miracles? If so many are cured, why are not all? Are the miraculÉs especially distinguished for piety? Is it to be expected that unbelievers will be convinced? Is it claimed that the evidence is irresistible? Let us go back to the Gospels. It used to be said by doubters that the "miraculous element" must have been added later by the piety of the disciples, because all the world knew now that "miracles" did not happen. That *a priori* argument is surely silenced by Lourdes. "Miracles" in that sense undoubtedly do happen, if present-day evidence is worth anything whatever. What, then, is the Christian theory?

It is this. Our Blessed Lord appears to have worked miracles of such a nature that their significance was not, historically speaking, absolutely evident to those who, for other reasons, did not "believe in Him." It is known how some asked for a "sign from heaven" and were refused it; how He Himself said that even if one rose from the dead, they would not believe; yet, further, how He begged them to believe Him even for His work's sake, if for nothing else. We know, finally, how, when confronted with one particular miracle, His enemies cried out that it must have been done by diabolical agency.

Very good, then. It would seem that the miracles of Our Lord were of a nature that strongly disposed to belief those that witnessed them, and helped vastly in the confirmation of the faith of those who already believed; but that miracles, as such, cannot absolutely compel the belief of those who for moral reasons refuse it. If they could, faith would cease to be faith.

Now, this seems precisely the state of affairs at Lourdes. Even unbelieving scientists are bound to admit that science at present cannot account for the facts, which is surely the modern equivalent for the Beelzebub theory. We have seen, too, how severely scientific persons such as Dr. Boissarie and Dr. Cox--if they will permit me to quote their names--knowing as well as anyone what medicine and surgery and hypnotism and suggestion can and cannot do, corroborate this evidence, and see in the facts a simple illustration of the truth of that Catholic Faith which they both hold and practise.

Is not the parallel a fair one? What more, then, do the adversaries want? There is no arguing with people who say that, since there is nothing but Nature, no process can be other than natural. There is no sign, even from heaven, that could break down the intellectual prejudice of such people. If they saw Jesus Christ Himself in glory, they could always say that "at present science cannot account for the phenomenon of a luminous body apparently seated upon a throne, but no doubt it will do so in the course of time." If they saw a dead and corrupting man rise from the grave, they could always argue that he could not have been dead and corrupting, or he could not have risen from the grave. Nothing but the Last Judgment could convince such persons. Even when the trumpet sounds, I believe that some of them, when they have recovered from their first astonishment, will make remarks about aural phenomena.

But for the rest of us, who believe in God and His Son and the Mother of God on quite other grounds--because our intellect is satisfied, our heart kindled, our will braced by the belief; and because without that belief all life falls into chaos, and human evidence is nullified, and all noble motive and emotion cease--for us, who have received the gift of faith, in however small a measure, Lourdes is enough. Christ and His Mother are with us. Jesus Christ is the same yesterday, to-day, and for ever. Is not that, after all, the simplest theory?

V.

After dÉjeÃ»ner I set out again to find the Scottish priest, who hoped to be able to take me to a certain window in the Rosary Church, where only a few were admitted, from which we might view the procession and the Blessing of the Sick. But we were disappointed; and, after a certain amount of scheming, we managed to get a position at the back of the crowd on the top of the church steps. I was able to climb up a few inches above the others, and secured a very tolerable view of the whole scene.

The crowd was beyond describing. Here about us was a vast concourse of men; and as far as the eye could reach down the huge oval, and far away beyond the crowned statue, and on either side back to the Bureau on the left, and on the slopes on the right, stretched an inconceivable pavement of heads. Above us, too, on every terrace and step, back to the doors of the great basilica, we knew very well, was one seething, singing mob. A great space was kept open on the level ground beneath us--I should say one hundred by two hundred yards in area--and the inside fringe of this was composed of the sick, in litters, in chairs, standing, sitting, lying and kneeling. It was at the farther end that the procession would enter.

After perhaps half an hour's waiting, during which one incessant gust of singing rolled this way and that through the crowd, the leaders of the procession appeared far away--little white or black figures, small as dolls--and the singing became general. But as the endless files rolled out, the singing ceased, and a moment later a priest, standing solitary in the great space began to pray aloud in a voice like a silver trumpet.

I have never heard such passion in my life. I began to watch presently, almost mechanically, the little group beneath the *ombrellino*, in white and gold, and the movements of the monstrance blessing the sick; but again and again my eyes wandered back to the little figure in the midst, and I cried out with the crowd, sentence after sentence, following that passionate voice:

"Seigneur, nous vous adorons!"

"Seigneur," came the huge response, "nous vous adorons!"

"Seigneur, nous vous aimons!" cried the priest.

"Seigneur, nous vous aimons!" answered the people.

"Sauvez-nous, JÉsus; nous pÉrissons!"

"Sauvez-nous, JÉsus; nous pÉrissons!"

"JÉsus, Fils de Marie, ayez pitiÉ de nous!"

"JÉsus, Fils de Marie, ayez pitiÉ de nous!"

Then with a surge rose up the plainsong melody.

"Parce, Domine!" sang the people. "Parce populo tuo! Ne in aeternum irascaris nobis."

Again:

"Gloria Patri et Filio et Spiritui Sancto."

"Sicut erat in principio et nunc et semper, et in sÃ!cula sÃ!culorum. Amen."

Then again the single voice and the multitudinous answer:

"Vous Ã\u00aates la RÉsurrection et la Vie!"

And then an adjuration to her whom He gave to be our Mother.

"MÈre du Sauveur, priez pour nous!"

"Salut des Infirmes, priez pour nous!"

Then once more the singing; then the cry, more touching than all:

"Seigneur, guÉrissez nos malades!"

"Seigneur, guÉrissez nos malades!"

Then the kindling shout that brought the blood to ten thousand faces:

"Hosanna! Hosanna au Fils de David!" (I shook to hear it).

"Hosanna!" cried the priest, rising from his knees with arms flung wide.

"Hosanna!" roared the people, swift as an echo.

"Hosanna! Hosanna!" crashed out again and again, like great artillery.

Yet there was no movement among those piteous prostrate lines. The Bishop, the ***ombrellino*** over him, passed on slowly round the circle; and the people cried to Him whom he bore, as they cried two thousand years ago on the road to the city of David. Surely He will be pitiful upon this day--the Jubilee Year of His Mother's graciousness, the octave of her assumption to sit with Him on His throne!

"MÈre du Sauveur, priez pour nous!"

"JÉsus, vous Ãªtes mon Seigneur et mon Dieu!"

Yet there was no movement.

If ever "suggestion" could work a miracle, it must work it now. "We expect the miracles during the procession to-morrow and on Sunday," a priest had said to me on the previous day. And there I stood, one of a hundred thousand, confident in expectation, thrilled by that voice, nothing doubting or fearing; there were the sick beneath me, answering weakly and wildly to the crying of the priest; and yet there was no movement, no sudden leap of a sick man from his bed as Jesus went by, no vibrating scream of joy--"Je suis guÉri! Je suis guÉri!"--no tumultuous rush to the place, and the roar of the *Magnificat*, as we had been led to expect.

The end was coming near now. The monstrance had reached the image once again, and was advancing down the middle. The voice of the priest grew more passionate still, as he tossed his arms and cried for mercy

"JÉsus, ayez pitiÉ de nous!--ayez pitiÉ[Transcriber's Note: original had "pitiÃª"] de nous!"

And the people, frantic with ardour and desire, answered him in a voice of thunder:

"Ayez pitiÉ de nous!--ayez pitiÉ de nous!"

And now up the steps came the grave group to where Jesus would at least bless His own, though He would not heal them; and the priest in the midst, with one last cry, gave glory to Him who must be served through whatever misery:

"Hosanna! Hosanna au Fils de David!"

Surely that must touch the Sacred Heart! Will not His Mother say one word?

"Hosanna! Hosanna au Fils de David!"

"Hosanna!" cried the priest.

"Hosanna!" cried the people.

"Hosanna! Hosanna! Hosanna!..."

One articulate roar of disappointed praise, and then--Tantum ergo Sacramentum! rose in its solemnity.

When Benediction was over, I went back to the Bureau; but there was little to be seen there. No, there were no miracles to-day, I was told--or hardly one. Perhaps one in the morning. It was not known.

Several Bishops were there again, listening to the talk of the doctors, and the description of certain cases on previous days. PÈre Salvator, the Capuchin, was there again; as also the tall bearded Assumptionist Father of whom I have spoken. But there was not a great deal of interest or excitement. I had the pleasure of talking a while with the Bishop of Tarbes, who introduced me again to the Capuchin, and retold his story.

But I was a little unhappy. The miracle was that I was not more so. I had expected so much: I had seen nothing.

I talked to Dr. Cox also before leaving.

"No," he told me, "there is hardly one miracle to-day. We are doubtful, too, about that leg that was seven centimetres too short."

"And is it true that Mademoiselle Bardou is not cured?" (A doctor had been giving us certain evidence a few minutes before).

"I am afraid so. It was probably a case of intense subjective excitement. But it may be an amelioration. We do not know yet. The real work of investigating comes afterwards."

How arbitrary it all seemed, I thought, as I walked home to dinner. That morning, on my way from the Bureau, I had seen a great company of white banners moving together; and, on inquiry, had found that these were the miraculÉs chiefly of previous years--about three hundred and fifty in number.[6] They formed a considerably large procession. I had looked at their faces: there were many more women than men (as there were upon Calvary). But as I watched them I could not conceive upon what principle the Supernatural had suddenly descended on this and not on that. "Two men in one bed.... Two women grinding at the mill.... One is taken and the other left." Here were persons of all ages--from six to eighty, I should guess--of all characters, ranks, experiences; of both sexes. Some were religious, some grocers, some of the nobility, a retired soldier or two, and so on. They were not distinguished for holiness, it seemed. I had heard heartbreaking little stories of the ten

---

6   The official numbers of those at the afternoon procession were 341.

lepers over again--one grateful, nine selfish. One or two of the girls, I heard, had had their heads turned by flattery and congratulation; they had begun to give themselves airs.

And, now again, here was this day, this almost obvious occasion. It was the Jubilee Year; everything was about on a double scale. And nothing had happened! Further, five of the sick had actually died at Lourdes during their first night there. To come so far and to die!

On what principle, then, did God act? Then I suddenly understood, not God's principles, but my own; and I went home both ashamed and comforted.

VI.

I said a midnight Mass that night in the same chapel of the Rosary Church as on the previous morning. Again the crush was terrific. On the steps of the church I saw a friar hearing a confession; and on entering I found High Mass proceeding in the body of the church itself, with a congregation so large and so worn-out that many were sleeping in constrained attitudes among the seats. In fact, I was informed, since the sleeping accommodation of Lourdes could not possibly provide for so large a pilgrimage, there were many hundreds, at least, who slept where they could--on the steps of churches, under trees and rocks, and by the banks of the river.

I was served at my Mass by a Scottish priest, immediately afterwards I served his at the same altar. While vesting, I noticed a priest at the high altar of this little chapel reading out acts of prayer, to which the congregation responded; and learned that two persons who had been received into the Church on that day were to make their First Communion. As midnight struck, simultaneously from the seven altars came seven voices:

"In nomine Patris, et Filii, et Spiritus Sancti. Amen."

Once more, on returning home and going to bed a little after one o'clock in the morning, the last sound that I heard was of the "Gloria Patri" being sung by other pilgrims also returning to their lodging.

After coffee, a few hours later, I went down again to the square. It was Sunday, and a Pontifical High Mass was being sung on the steps of the Rosary Church. As usual, the crowd filled the square, and I could hardly penetrate for a while beyond the fringe; but it was a new experience to hear that vast congregation in the open air responding with one giant voice to the plain-song of the Mass. It was astonishing what expression showed itself in the singing. The *Sanctus* was one of the most impressive peals of worship and adoration that I have ever heard. At the close of the Mass, all the bishops present near the altar--I counted six or seven--turned and gave the blessing simultaneously. On the two great curves that led up to the basilica were grouped the white banners of the miraculÉs.

Soon after arriving at the Bureau a very strange and quiet little incident happened. A woman with a yellowish face, to which the colour was slowly returning, came in and sat down to give her evidence. She declared to us that during the procession yesterday she had been cured of a tumour on the liver. She had suddenly experienced an overwhelming sense of relief, and had walked home completely restored to health. On being asked why she did not present herself at the Bureau, she answered that she did not think of it: she had just gone home. I have not yet heard whether this was a true cure or not; all I can say at present is I was as much impressed by her simple and natural bearing, her entire self-possession, and the absence of excitement, as by anything I saw at Lourdes. I cannot conceive such a woman suffering from an illusion.

A few minutes later Dr. Cox called to me, and writing on a card, handed it to me, telling me it would admit me to the *piscines* for a bath. I had asked for this previously; but had been told it was not certain, owing to the crush of patients, whether it could be granted. I set out immediately to the *piscines*.

There are, as I have said, three compartments in the building called the *piscines*. That on the left is for women; in the middle, for children and for those who do not undergo complete immersion; on the right, for men. It was into this last, then, that I went, when I had forced my way through the crowd, and passed the open court where the priests prayed. It was a little paved place like a chapel, with a curtain hung immediately before the door. When I had passed this, I saw at the farther end, three or four yards away, was a deepish trough, wide and long enough to hold one person. Steps went down on either side of it, for the attendants. Immediately above the bath, on the wall, was a statue of Our Lady; and beneath it a placard of prayers, large enough to be read at a little distance.

There were about half a dozen people in the place--two or three priests and three or four patients. One of the priests, I was relieved to see, was the Scotsman whose Mass I had served the previous midnight. He was in his soutane, with his sleeves rolled up to the elbow. He gave me my directions, and while I made ready I watched the patients. There was one lame man, just beside me, beginning to dress; two tiny boys, and a young man who touched me more than I can say. He was standing by the head of the bath, holding a basin in one hand and a little image of our Lady in the other, and was splashing water ingeniously with his fingers into his eyes; these were horribly inflamed, and I could see that he was blind. I cannot describe the passion with which he did this, seeming to stare all the while towards the image he held, and whispering out prayers in a quick undertone--hoping, no doubt, that his first sight would be the image of his Mother. Then I looked at the boys. One of them had horribly prolonged and thin legs; I could not see what was wrong with the other, except that he looked ill and worn out. Close beside me, on the wet, muddy paving, lay an indescribable bandage that had been unrolled from the lame man's leg.

When my turn came, I went wrapped in a soaking apron, down a step or so into the water; and then, with a priest holding either hand, lay down at full length so that my head only emerged. That water had better not be described. It is enough to say that people suffering from most of the diseases known to man had bathed in it without ceasing for at least five or six hours. Yet I can say, with entire sincerity, that I did not have even the faintest physical repulsion, though commonly I hate dirt at least as much as sin. It is said, too, that never in the history of Lourdes has there been one case of disease traceable to infection from the baths. The water was cold, but not unpleasantly. I lay there, I suppose, about one minute, while the two priests and myself repeated off the placard the prayers inscribed there. These were, for the most part, petitions to Mary to pray. "O Marie," they ended, "conÃ§ue sans pÉchÉ, priez pour nous qui avons recours a vous!"

As I dressed again after the bath, I had one more sight of the young man. He was being led out by a kindly attendant, but his face was all distorted with crying, and from his blind eyes ran down a stream of terrible tears. It is unnecessary to say that I said a "Hail Mary" for his soul at least.

As soon as I was ready, I went out and sat down for a while among the recently bathed, and began to remind myself why *I* had bathed. Certainly I was not suffering from anything except a negligible ailment or two. Neither did I do it out of curiosity, because I could have seen without difficulty all the details without descending into that appalling trough. I suppose it was just an act of devotion. Here was water with a history behind it; water that was as undoubtedly used by Almighty God for giving benefits to man as was the clay laid upon blind eyes long ago near Siloe, or the water of Bethesda itself. And it is a natural instinct to come as close as possible to things used by the heavenly powers. I was extraordinarily glad I had bathed, and I have been equally glad ever since. I am afraid it is of no use as evidence to say that until I came to Lourdes I was tired out, body and mind; and that since my return I have been unusually robust. Yet that is a fact, and I leave it there.

As I sat there a procession went past to the Grotto, and I walked to the railings to look at it. I do not know at all what it was all about, but it was as impressive as all things are in Lourdes. The miraculÉs came first with their banners--file after file of them--then a number of prelates, then *brancardiers* with their shoulder-harness, then nuns, then more *brancardiers*. I think perhaps they may have been taking a recent miraculÉ to give thanks; for when I arrived presently at the Bureau again, I heard that, after all, several appeared to have been cured at the procession on the previous day.

I was sitting in the hall of the hotel a few minutes later when I heard the roar of the *Magnificat* from the street, and ran out to see what was forward. As I came to the door, the heart of the procession went by. A group of *brancardiers* formed an irregular square, holding cords to keep back the crowd; and in the middle walked a group of three, followed by an empty litter. The three were a white-haired man on this side, a stalwart *brancardier* on the other, and between them a girl with a radiant face, singing with all her heart. She had been carried down from her lodging that morning to the *piscines*; she was returning on her own feet, by the power of Him who said to the lame man, "Take up thy bed and go into thy house." I followed them a little way, then I went back to the hotel.

VII.

In the afternoon we went down to meet a priest who had promised a place to one of our party in the window of which I have spoken before. But the crowd was so great that we could not find him, so presently we dispersed as best we could. Two other priests and myself went completely round the outside of the churches, in order, if possible, to join in the procession, since to cross the square was a simple impossibility. In the terrible crush near the Bureau, I became separated from the others, and fought my way back, and into the Bureau, as the best place open to me now for seeing the Blessing of the Sick.

It was now at last that I had my supreme wish. Within a minute or two of my coming to look through the window, the Blessed Sacrament entered the reserved space among the countless litters. The crowd between me and the open space was simply one pack of heads; but I could observe the movements of what was going forward by the white top of the ***ombrellino*** as it passed slowly down the farther side of the square.

The crowd was very still, answering as before the passionate voice in the midst; but watching, watching, as I watched. Beside me sat Dr. Cox, and our Rosaries were in our hands. The white spot moved on and on, and all else was motionless. I knew that beyond it lay the sick. "Lord, if it be possible--if it be possible! Nevertheless, not my will but Thine be done." It had reached now the end of the first line.

"Seigneur, guÉrissez nos malades!" cried the priest.

"Seigneur, guÉrissez nos malades!" answered the people.

"Vous Ãªtes mon Seigneur et mon Dieu!"

And then on a sudden it came.

Overhead lay the quiet summer air, charged with the Supernatural as a cloud with thunder--electric, vibrating with power. Here beneath lay souls thirsting for its touch of fire--patient, desirous, infinitely pathetic; and in the midst that Power, incarnate for us men and our salvation. Then it descended, swift and mighty.

I saw a sudden swirl in the crowd of heads beneath the church steps, and then a great shaking ran through the crowd; but there for a few instants it boiled like a pot. A sudden cry had broken out, and it ran through the whole space; waxing in volume as it ran, till the heads beneath my window shook with it also; hands clapped, voices shouted: "Un miracle! Un miracle!"

I was on my feet, staring and crying out. Then quietly the shaking ceased, and the shouting died to a murmur; and the **ombrellino** moved on; and again the voice of the priest thrilled thin and clear, with a touch of triumphant thankfulness: "Vous Ãªtes la RÉsurrection et la Vie!" And again, with entreaty once more--since there still were two thousand sick untouched by that Power, and time pressed--that infinitely moving plea: "Seigneur, celui qui vous aime est malade!" And: "Seigneur, faites que je marche! Seigneur, faites que j'entende!"

And then again the finger of God flashed down, and again and again; and each time a sick and broken body sprang from its bed of pain and stood upright; and the crowd smiled and roared and sobbed. Five times I saw that swirl and rush; the last when the **Te Deum** pealed out from the church steps as Jesus in His Sacrament came home again. And there were two that I did not see. There were seven in all that afternoon.

Now, is it of any use to comment on all this? I am not sure; and yet, for my own satisfaction if for no one else's, I wish to set down some of the thoughts that came to me both then and after I had sat at the window and seen God's loving-kindness with my own eyes.

The first overwhelming impression that remained with me is this--that I had been present, in my own body, in the twentieth century, and seen Jesus pass along by the sick folk, as He passed two thousand years before. That, in a word, is the supreme fact of Lourdes. More than once as I sat there that afternoon I contrasted the manner in which I was spending it with that in which the average believing Christian spends Sunday afternoon. As a child, I used to walk with my father, and he used to read and talk on religious subjects; on our return we used to have a short Bible-class in his study. As an Anglican clergyman, I used to teach in Sunday schools or preach to children. As a Catholic priest, I used occasionally to attend at catechism. At all these times the miraculous seemed singularly far away; we looked at it across twenty centuries; it was something from which lessons might be drawn, upon which the imagination might feed, but it was a state of affairs as remote as the life of prehistoric man; one assented to it, and that was all. And here at Lourdes it was a present, vivid event. I sat at an ordinary glass window, in a soutane made by an English tailor, with another Englishman beside me, and saw the miraculous happen. Time and space disappeared; the centuries shrank and vanished; and behold we saw that which "prophets and kings have desired to see and have not seen!"

Of course "scientific" arguments, of the sort which I have related, can be brought forward in an attempt to explain Lourdes; but they are the same arguments that can be, and are, brought forward against the miracles of Jesus Christ Himself. I say nothing to those here; I leave that to scientists such as Dr. Boissarie; but what I cannot understand is that professing Christians are able to bring *a priori* arguments against the fact that Our Lord is the same yesterday, to-day, and for ever-- the same in Galilee and in France. "These signs shall follow them that believe," He said Himself; and the history of the Catholic Church is an exact fulfilment of the words. It was so, St. Augustine tells us, at the tombs of the martyrs; five hundred miracles were reported at Canterbury within a few years of St. Thomas' martyrdom. And now here is Lourdes, as it has been for fifty years, in this little corner of poor France!

I have been asked since my return: "Why cannot miracles be done in England?" My answer is, firstly, that they are done in England, in Liverpool, and at Holywell, for example; secondly, I answer by another question as to why Jesus Christ was not born in Rome; and if He had been born in Rome, why not in Nineveh and Jerusalem? Thirdly, I answer that perhaps more would be done in England, if there were more faith there. It is surely a little unreasonable to ask that, in a country which three hundred and fifty years ago deliberately repudiated Christ's Revelation of Himself, banished the Blessed Sacrament and tore down Mary's shrines, Christ and His Mother should cooperate supernaturally in marvels that are rather the rewards of the faithful. "It is not meet to take the children's bread and to cast it to the dogs"- -these are the words of our Lord Himself. If London is not yet tolerant enough to allow an Eucharistic Procession in her streets, she is scarcely justified in demanding that our Eucharistic Lord should manifest His power. "He could do no mighty work there," says the Evangelist, of Capharnaum, "because of their unbelief."

This, then, is the supreme fact of Lourdes: that Jesus Christ in His Sacrament passes along that open square, with the sick laid in beds on either side; and that at His word the lame walk and lepers are cleansed and deaf hear--that they are seen leaping and dancing for joy.

Even now, writing within ten days of my return, all seems like a dream; and yet I know that I saw it. For over thirty years I had been accustomed to repeat the silly formula that "the age of miracles is past"; that they were necessary for the establishment of Christianity, but that they are no longer necessary now, except on extremely rare occasions perhaps; and in my heart I knew my foolishness. Why, for those thirty years Lourdes had been in existence! And if I spoke of it at all, I spoke only of hysteria and auto-suggestion and French imaginativeness, and the rest of the nonsense. It is impossible for a Christian who has been at Lourdes to speak like that again.

And as for the unreality, that does not trouble me. I have no doubt that those who saw the bandages torn from the leper's limbs and the sound flesh shown beneath, or the once blind man, his eyes now dripping with water of Siloe, looking on Him who had made him whole, or heard the marvellous talk of "men like trees walking," and the rest--I have no doubt that ten days later they sat themselves with unseeing eyes, and wondered whether it was indeed they who had witnessed those things. Human nature, like a Leyden jar, cannot hold beyond a fixed quantity; and this human nature, with experience, instincts, education, common talk, public opinion, and all the rest of it, echoing round it; the assumption that miracles *do not happen*; that laws are laws; in other words, that Deism is the best that can be hoped--well, it is little wonder that the visible contradiction of all this conventionalism finds but little room in the soul.

Then there is another point that I should like to make in the presence of "Evangelical" Christians who shake their heads over Mary's part in the matter. It is this--that for every miracle that takes place in the *piscines*, I should guess that a dozen take place while That which we believe to be Jesus Christ goes by. Catholics, naturally, need no such reassurance; they know well enough from interior experience that when Mary comes forward Jesus does not retire! But for those who think as some Christians do, it is necessary to point out the facts. And again. I have before me as I write the little card of ejaculations that are used in the procession. There are twenty-four in all. Of these, twenty-one are addressed to Jesus Christ; in two more we ask the "Mother of the Saviour" and the "Health of the Sick" to pray for us; in the last we ask her to "show herself a Mother." If people will talk of "proportion" in a matter in which there is no such thing--since there can be no comparison, without grave irreverence, between the Creator and a creature--I would ask, Is there "disproportion" here?

In fact, Lourdes, as a whole, is an excellent little compendium of Catholic theology and Gospel-truth. There was once a marriage feast, and the Mother of Jesus was there with her Son. There was no wine. She told her Son what He already knew; He seemed to deprecate her words; but He obeyed them, and the water became wine.

There is at Lourdes not a marriage feast, but something very like a deathbed. The Mother of Jesus is there with her Son. It is she again who takes the initiative. "Here is water," she seems to say; "dig, Bernadette, and you will find it." But it is no more than water. Then she turns to her Son. "They have water," she says, "but no more." And then He comes forth in His power. "Draw out now from all the sick beds of the world and bear them to the Governor of the Feast. Use the commonest things in the world--physical pain and common water. Bring them together, and wait until I pass by." Then Jesus of Nazareth passes by; and the sick leap from their beds, and the blind see, and the lepers are cleansed, and devils are cast out.

Oh, yes! the parallel halts; but is it not near enough?

Seigneur, guÉrissez nos malades!

Salut des Infirmes, priez pour nous!

VIII.

The moment Benediction was given, the room began rapidly to fill; but I still watched the singing crowd outside. Among others I noticed a woman, placid and happy--such a woman as you would see a hundred times a day in London streets, with jet ornaments in her hat, middle-aged, almost startlingly commonplace. No, nothing dramatic happened to her; that was the point. But there she was, taking it all for granted, joining in the *Magnificat* with a roving eye, pleased as she would have been pleased at a circus; interrupting herself to talk to her neighbour; and all the while gripping in a capable hand, on which shone a wedding ring, the bars of the Bureau window behind which I sat, that she might make the best of both worlds--Grace without and Science within. She, as I, had seen what God had done; now she proposed to see what the doctors would make of it all; and have, besides, a good view of the miraculÉs when they appeared.

I suppose it was her astonishing ordinariness that impressed me. It was surprising to see such a one during such a scene; it was as incongruous as a man riding a bicycle on the judgment Day. Yet she, too, served to make it all real. She was like the real tree in the foreground of a panorama. She served the same purpose as the *Voix de Lourdes*, a briskly written French newspaper that gives the lists of the miracles.

When I turned round at last, the room was full. Among the people present I remember an Hungarian canon, and the Brazilian Bishop with six others. Dr. Deschamps, late of Lille, now of Paris, was in the chair; and I sat next him.

The first patient to enter was Euphrasie Bosc, a dark girl of twenty-seven. She rolled a little in her walk as she came in; then she sat down and described the "white swellings" on her knee, with other details; she told how she had been impelled to rise during the procession just now. She was made to walk round the room to show her state, and was then sent off, and told to return at another time.

Next came Emma Sansen, a pale girl of twenty-five. She had suffered from endo-pericarditis for five years, as her certificate showed; she had been confined to her room for two years. She told her story quickly and went out.

There followed Sister MarguÉrite Emilie, an Assumptionist, aged thirty-nine, a brisk, brown-faced, tall woman, in her religious habit. Her malady had been ***mal de Pott***, a severe spinal affliction, accompanied by abscesses and other horrors. She, too, appeared in the best of health.

We began then to hear a doctor give news of a certain Irish Religious, cured that morning in the ***piscines***; but we were interrupted by the entry of Emile Lansman, a solid artisan of twenty-five who came in walking cheerfully, carrying a crutch and a stick which he no longer needed. Paralysis of the right leg and traumatism of the spine had been his, up to that day. Now he carried his crutch.

He was followed by another man whose name I did not catch, and on whose case I wrote so rapidly that I am scarcely able to read all my notes. His story, in brief, was as follows. He had had some while ago a severe accident, which involved a kind of appalling disembowelment. For the last year or two he had had gastric troubles of all kinds, including complete loss of appetite. His certificate showed too, that he suffered from partial paralysis (he himself showed us how little he had been able to open his fingers), and anÃⁱsthesia of the right arm. (I looked over Dr. Deschamps' shoulder and read on the paper the words lÉsion incurable). It was certified further that he was incapable of manual work. Then he described to us how yesterday in the ***piscine***, upon coming out of the bath, he had been aware of a curious sensation of warmth in the stomach; he had then found that, for the first time for many months, he wished for food; he was given it, and he enjoyed it. He moved his fingers in a normal manner, raised his arm and let it fall.

Then for the first time in the Bureau I heard a sharp controversy. One doctor suddenly broke out, saying that there was no actual proof that it was not all "hysterical simulation." Another answered him; an appeal was made to the certificate. Then the first doctor delivered a little speech, in excellent taste, though casting doubt upon the case; and the matter was then set aside for investigation with the rest. I heard Dr. Boissarie afterwards thank him for his admirable little discourse.

Finally, though it was getting late, Honorie Gras, aged thirty-five, came in to give her evidence. She had suffered till to-day from "purulent arthritis" and "white swellings" on the left knee. To-day she walked. Her certificate confirmed her, and she was dismissed.

It was all very matter-of-fact. There is no reason to fear that Lourdes is all hymn-singing and adjurations. It is a pleasure to think that, on the right of the Rosary Church, and within a hundred yards of the Grotto, there is this little room, filled with keen-eyed doctors from every school of faith and science, who have only to present their cards and be made free of all that Lourdes has to show. They are keen-brained as well as keen-eyed. I heard one of them say quietly that if the Mother of God, as it appeared, cured incurable cases, it was hard to deny to her the power of curing curable cases also. It does not prove, that is to say, that a cure is not miraculous, if it might have been cured by human aid. And it is interesting and suggestive to remember that of such cases one hears little or nothing. For every startling miracle that is verified in the Bureau, I wonder how many persons go home quietly, freed from some maddening little illness by the mercy of Mary--some illness that is worthless as a "case" in scientific eyes, yet none the less as real as is its cure?

Of course one element that tends to keep from the grasp of the imagination all the miracles of the place is all this scientific phraseology. In the simple story of the Gospel, it seems almost supernaturally natural that a man should have "lain with an infirmity for forty years," and should, at the word of Jesus Christ, have taken up his bed and walked; or that, as in the "Acts," another's "feet and ankle-bones should receive strength" by the power of the Holy Name. But when we come to tuberculosis and ***mal de Pott*** and lÉsion incurable and "hysterical simulation," in some manner we seem to find ourselves in rather a breathless and stuffy room, where the white flower of the supernatural appears strangely languid to the eye of the imagination.

That, however, is all as it should be. We are bound to have these things. Perhaps the most startling miracle of all is that the Bureau and the Grotto stand side by side, and that neither stifles the other. Is it possible that here at last Science and Religion will come to terms, and each confess with wonder the capacities of the other, and, with awe, that divine power that makes them what they are, and has "set them their bounds which they shall not pass?" It would be remarkable if France, of all countries, should be the scene of that reconciliation between these estranged sisters.

That night, after dinner, I went out once more to see the procession with torches; and this time my friend and I each took a candle, that we might join in that act of worship. First, however, I went down to the ***robinets***--the taps which flow between the Grotto and the ***piscines***--and, after a heartcrushing struggle, succeeded in filling my bottle with the holy water. It was astonishing how selfish one felt while still in the battle, and how magnanimous when one had gained the victory. I filled also the bottle of a voluble French priest, who despairingly extended it toward me as he still fought in the turmoil. "Eh, bien!" cried a stalwart Frenchwoman at my side, who had filled her bottle and could not extricate herself. "If you will not permit me to depart, I remain!" The argument was irresistible; the crowd laughed childishly and let her out.

Now, I regret to say that once more the churches were outlined in fairy electric lamps, that the metallic garlands round our Mother's statue blazed with them; that, even worse, the old castle on the hill and the far away Calvary were also illuminated; and, worst of all, that the procession concluded with fireworks--rockets and bombs. Miracles in the afternoon; fireworks in the evening!

Yet the more I think of it, the less am I displeased. When one reflects that more than half of the enormous crowd came, probably, from tiny villages in France--where a rocket is as rare as an angelic visitation; and, on the carnal side, as beautiful in their eyes--it seems a very narrow-minded thing to object. It is true that you and I connect fireworks with Mafeking night or Queen Victoria's Jubilee; and that they seem therefore incongruous when used to celebrate a visitation of God. But it is not so with these people. For them it is a natural and beautiful way of telling the glory of Him who is the Dayspring from on high, who is the Light to lighten the Gentiles, whose Mother is the ***Stella Matutina***, whose people once walked in darkness and now have seen a great Light. It is their answer--the reflection in the depths of their sea--to the myriad lights of that heaven which shines over Lourdes. Therefore let us leave the fireworks in peace.

It was a very moving thing to walk in that procession, with a candle in one hand and a little paper book in the other, and help to sing the story of Bernadette, with the unforgettable ***Aves*** at the end of each verse, and the ***Laudate Mariam***, and the Nicene Creed. ***Credo in ... unam sanctam Catholicam et Apostolicam Ecclesiam.*** My heart leaped at that. For where else but in the Catholic Church do such things happen as these that I had seen? Imagine, if you please, miracles in Manchester! Certainly they might happen there, if there were sufficient Catholics gathered in His Name; but put for Manchester, Exeter Hall or St. Paul's Cathedral! The thought is blindingly absurd. No; the Christianity of Jesus Christ lives only in the Catholic Church.

There alone in the whole round world do you find that combination of lofty doctrine, magnificent moral teaching, the frank recognition of the Cross; sacramentalism logically carried out, yet gripping the heart as no amateur mysticism can do; and miracles. "Mercy and Truth have met together." "These signs shall follow them that believe.... Faith can remove mountains.... All things are possible to him that believes.... Whatsoever you shall ask of the Father in My Name.... Where two or three are gathered together in My Name, there am I in the midst of them." There alone, where souls are built upon Peter, do these things really happen.

I have been asked lately whether I am "happy" in the Catholic Church. Happy! What can one say to a question like that? Does one ask a man who wakes up from a foolish dream to sunshine in his room, and to life and reality, whether he is happy? Of course many non-Catholics are happy. I was happy myself as an Anglican; but as a Catholic one does not use the word; one does not think about it. The whole of life is different; that is all that can be said. Faith is faith, not hope; God is Light, not twilight; eternity, heaven, hell, purgatory, sin and its consequences--these things are facts, not guesses and conjectures and suspicions desperately clung to. "How hard it is to be a Christian!" moans the persevering non-Catholic. "How impossible it is to be anything else!" cries the Catholic.

We went round, then, singing. The procession was so huge that it seemed to have no head and no tail. It involved itself a hundred times over; it swirled in the square, it humped itself over the Rosary Church; it elongated itself half a mile away up beyond our Mother's garlanded statue; it eddied round the Grotto. It was one immense pool and river of lights and song. Each group sang by itself till it was overpowered by another; men and women and children strolled along patiently singing and walking, knowing nothing of where they went, nothing of what they would be singing five minutes hence. It depended on the voice-power of their neighbours.

For myself, I found myself in a dozen groups, before, at last, after an hour or so, I fell out of the procession and went home. Now I walked cheek by jowl with a retired officer; now with an artisan; once there came swiftly up behind a company of "Noelites"--those vast organizations of boys and girls in France--singing the ***Laudate Mariam*** to my ***Ave Maria***; now in the middle of a group of shop-girls who exchanged remarks with one another whenever they could fetch breath. I think it was all the most joyous and the most spontaneous (as it was certainly the largest) human function in which I have ever taken part. I have no idea whether there were any organizers of it all--at least I saw none. Once or twice a solitary priest in the midst, walking backward and waving his arms, attempted to reconcile conflicting melodies; once a very old priest; with a voice like the tuba stop on the organ, turned a humorously furious face over his shoulder to quell some mistake--from his mouth, the while issuing this amazingly pungent volume of sound. But I think these were the only attempts at organization that I saw.

And so at last I dropped out and went home, hoarse but very well content. I had walked for more than an hour--from the statue, over the lower church and down again, up the long avenue, and back again to the statue. The fireworks were over, the illuminations died, and the day was done; yet still the crowds went round and the voice of conflicting melody went up without cessation. As I went home the sound was still in my ears. As I dropped off to sleep, I still heard it.

IX.

Next morning I awoke with a heavy heart, for we were to leave in the motor at half-past eight, I had still a few errands to do, and had made no arrangements for saying Mass; so I went out quickly, a little after seven, and up to the Rosary Church to get some pious objects blessed. It was useless: I could not find the priest of whom I had been told, whose business it is perpetually to bless such things. I went to the basilica, then round by the hill-path down to the Grotto, where I became wedged suddenly and inextricably into a silent crowd.

For a while I did not understand what they were doing beyond hearing Mass; for I knew that, of course, a Mass was proceeding just round the corner in the cave. But presently I perceived that these were intending communicants. So I made what preparation I could, standing there; and thanked God and His Mother for this unexpected opportunity of saying good-bye in the best way--for I was as sad as a schoolboy going the rounds of the house on Black Monday--and after a quarter of an hour or so I was kneeling at the grill, beneath the very image of Mary. After making my thanksgiving, still standing on the other side, I blessed the objects myself--strictly against all rules, I imagine--and came home to breakfast; and before nine we were on our way.

We were all silent as we progressed slowly and carefully through the crowded streets, seeing once more the patient *brancardiers* and the pitiful litters on their way to the *piscines*. I could not have believed that I could have become so much attached to a place in three summer days. As I have said before, everything was against it. There was no leisure, no room to move, no silence, no sense of familiarity. All was hot and noisy and crowded and dusty and unknown. Yet I felt that it was such a home of the soul as I never visited before--of course it is a home, for it is the Mother that makes the home.

We saw no more of the Grotto nor the churches nor the square nor the statue. Our road led out in such a direction that, after leaving the hotel, we had only commonplace streets, white houses, shops, hotels and crowds; and soon we had passed from the very outskirts of the town, and were beginning with quickening speed to move out along one of those endless straight roads that are the glory of France's locomotion.

Yet I turned round in my seat, sick at heart, and pulled the blind that hung over the rear window of the car. No, Lourdes was gone! There was the ring of the eternal hills, blue against the blue summer sky, with their shades of green beneath sloping to the valleys, and the rounded bastions that hold them up. The Gave was gone, the churches gone, the Grotto--all was gone. Lourdes might be a dream of the night.

No, Lourdes was not gone. For there, high on a hill, above where the holy city lay, stood the cross we had seen first upon our entrance, telling us that if health is a gift of God, it is not the greatest; that the Physician of souls, who healed the sick, and without whom not one sparrow falls to the ground, and not one pang is suffered, Himself had not where to lay His head, and died in pain upon the Tree.

And even as I looked we wheeled a corner, and the cross was gone.

*   *   *   *   *

How is it possible to end such a story without bathos? I think it is not possible, yet I must end it. An old French priest said one day at Lourdes, to one of those with whom I travelled, that he feared that in these times the pilgrims did not pray so much as they once did, and that this was a bad sign. He spoke also of France as a whole, and its fall. My friend said to him that, in her opinion, if these pilgrims could but be led as an army to Paris--an army, that is, with no weapons except their Rosaries--the country could be retaken in a day.

Now, I do not know whether the pilgrims once prayed more than they do now; I only know that I never saw any one pray so much; and I cannot help agreeing with my friend that, if this power could be organized, we should hear little more of the apostasy of France. Even as it is, I cannot understand the superior attitude that

Christian Englishmen take up with regard to France. It is true that in many districts religion is on a downward course, that the churches are neglected, and that even infidelity is becoming a fashion;[7] but I wonder very much whether, on the whole, taking Lourdes into account, the average piety of France, is not on a very much higher level than the piety of England. The government, as all the world now knows, is not in the least representative of the country; but, sad to relate, the Frenchman is apt to extend his respect for the law into an assumption of its morality. When a law is passed, there is an end of it.

Yet, judging by the intensity of faith and love and resignation that is evident at Lourdes, and indeed by the numbers of those present, it would seem as if Mary, driven from the towns with her Divine Son, has chosen Lourdes--the very farthest point from Paris--as her earthly home, and draws her children after her, standing there with her back to the wall. I do not think this is fanciful. That which is beyond time and space must communicate with us in those terms; and we can only speak of these things in the same terms. Huysmans expresses the same thing in other words. Even if Bernadette were deceived, he says, at any rate these pilgrims are not; even if Mary did not come in 1858 to the banks of the Gave, she has certainly come there since, drawn by the thousands of souls that have gone to seek her there.

This, then, is the last thing I can say about Lourdes. It is quite useless as evidence--indeed it would be almost impertinent to dare to offer further evidence at all--yet I may as well hand it in as my contribution. It is this, ***that Lourdes is soaked, saturated and kindled by the all but sensible presence of the Mother of God***. I am quite aware of all that can be said about subjectivity and auto-suggestion, and the rest; but there comes a point in all arguments when nothing is worth anything except an assertion of a personal conviction. Such, then, is mine.

First, it was borne in upon me what a mutilated Christianity that is which practically takes no account of Mary. This fragmentary, lopsided faith was that in which I myself had been brought up, and which to-day still is the faith of the majority of my fellow-countrymen. The Mother of God--the Second Eve, the Immaculate Maiden Mother, who, as if to balance Eve at the Tree of Death, stood by the Tree of Life--in popular non-Catholic theology is banished, with the rest of those who

---

7   It must be remembered that this was written six years ago, and is no longer true.

have passed away, to a position of complete insignificance. This arrangement, I had become accustomed to believe, was that of Primitive Christianity and of the Christianity of all sensible men: Romanism had added to the simple Gospel, and had treated the Mother of God with an honour which she would have been the first to deprecate.

Well, I think that at Lourdes the startling contrast between facts and human inventions was, in this respect, first made vivid to my imagination. I understood how puzzling it must be for "old Catholics," to whom Mary is as real and active as her Divine Son, to understand the sincerity of those to whom she is no more than a phantom, and who yet profess and call themselves Christians. Why, at Lourdes Mary is seen to stand, to all but outward eyes, in exactly that position in which at Nazareth, at Cana, in the Acts of the Apostles, in the Catacombs, and in the whole history of Christendom, true lovers of her Son have always seen her--a Mother of God and man, tender, authoritative, silent, and effective!

Yet, strangely enough, it is not at all the ordinary and conventional character of a merely tender mother that reveals itself at Lourdes--one who is simply desirous of relieving pain and giving what is asked. There comes upon one instead the sense of a tremendous personage--Regina CÅ"li as well as ***Consolatrix Afflictorum***--one who says "No" as well as "Yes," and with the same serenity; yet with the "No" gives strength to receive it. I have heard it said that the greatest miracle of all at Lourdes is the peace and resignation, even the happiness, of those who, after expectation has been wrought to the highest, go disappointed away, as sick as they came. Certainly that is an amazing fact. The tears of the young man in the ***piscine*** were the only tears of sorrow I saw at Lourdes.

Mary, then, has appeared to me in a new light since I have visited Lourdes. I shall in future not only hate to offend her, but fear it also. It is a fearful thing to fall into the hands of that Mother who allows the broken sufferer to crawl across France to her feet--and then to crawl back again. She is one of the Maries of Chartres, that reveals herself here, dark, mighty, dominant, and all but inexorable; not the Mary of an ecclesiastical shop, who dwells amid tinsel and tuberoses. She is Sedes Sapi-entiÃ¦, ***Turris Eburnea***, ***Virgo Paritura***, strong and tall and glorious, pierced by seven swords, yet serene as she looks to her Son.

Yet, at the same time, the tenderness of her great heart shows itself at Lourdes almost beyond bearing. She is so great and so loving! It affects those to whom one speaks--the quiet doctors, even those who, through some confusion of mind or some sin, find it hard to believe; the strong **brancardiers**, who carry their quivering burdens with such infinite care; the very sick themselves, coming back from the **piscines** in agony, yet with the faces of those who come down from the altar after Holy Communion. The whole place is alive with Mary and the love of God--from the inadequate statue at the Grotto to the brazen garlands in the square, even as far as the illuminated castle and the rockets that burst and bang against the steady stars. If I were sick of some deadly disease, and it were revealed to me that I must die, yet none the less I should go to Lourdes; for if I should not be healed by Mary, I could at least learn how to suffer as a Christian ought. God has chosen this place--He only knows why, as He, too, alone chooses which man shall suffer and which be glad--He has chosen this place to show His power; and therefore has sent His Mother there, that we may look through her to Him.

Is this, then, all subjectivity and romantic dreaming? Well, but there are the miracles!

The Codes Of Hammurabi And Moses
W. W. Davies

QTY

The discovery of the Hammurabi Code is one of the greatest achievements of archaeology, and is of paramount interest, not only to the student of the Bible, but also to all those interested in ancient history...

Religion **ISBN:** *1-59462-338-4*

Pages:132
MSRP $12.95

The Theory of Moral Sentiments
Adam Smith

QTY

This work from 1749. contains original theories of conscience amd moral judgment and it is the foundation for systemof morals.

Philosophy ISBN: *1-59462-777-0*

Pages:536
MSRP $19.95

Jessica's First Prayer
Hesba Stretton

QTY

In a screened and secluded corner of one of the many railway-bridges which span the streets of London there could be seen a few years ago, from five o'clock every morning until half past eight, a tidily set-out coffee-stall, consisting of a trestle and board, upon which stood two large tin cans, with a small fire of charcoal burning under each so as to keep the coffee boiling during the early hours of the morning when the work-people were thronging into the city on their way to their daily toil...

Childrens ISBN: *1-59462-373-2*

Pages:84
MSRP $9.95

My Life and Work
Henry Ford

QTY

Henry Ford revolutionized the world with his implementation of mass production for the Model T automobile. Gain valuable business insight into his life and work with his own auto-biography... "We have only started on our development of our country we have not as yet, with all our talk of wonderful progress, done more than scratch the surface. The progress has been wonderful enough but..."

Biographies/ ISBN: *1-59462-198-5*

Pages:300
MSRP $21.95

The Art of Cross-Examination
Francis Wellman

QTY

I presume it is the experience of every author, after his first book is published upon an important subject, to be almost overwhelmed with a wealth of ideas and illustrations which could readily have been included in his book, and which to his own mind, at least, seem to make a second edition inevitable. Such certainly was the case with me; and when the first edition had reached its sixth impression in five months, I rejoiced to learn that it seemed to my publishers that the book had met with a sufficiently favorable reception to justify a second and considerably enlarged edition. ..

Reference   ISBN: *1-59462-647-2*

Pages:412

MSRP $19.95

On the Duty of Civil Disobedience
Henry David Thoreau

QTY

Thoreau wrote his famous essay, On the Duty of Civil Disobedience, as a protest against an unjust but popular war and the immoral but popular institution of slave-owning. He did more than write—he declined to pay his taxes, and was hauled off to gaol in consequence. Who can say how much this refusal of his hastened the end of the war and of slavery ?

Law   ISBN: *1-59462-747-9*

Pages:48

MSRP $7.45

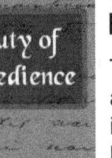

Dream Psychology Psychoanalysis for Beginners
Sigmund Freud

QTY

Sigmund Freud, born Sigismund Schlomo Freud (May 6, 1856 - September 23, 1939), was a Jewish-Austrian neurologist and psychiatrist who co-founded the psychoanalytic school of psychology. Freud is best known for his theories of the unconscious mind, especially involving the mechanism of repression; his redefinition of sexual desire as mobile and directed towards a wide variety of objects; and his therapeutic techniques, especially his understanding of transference in the therapeutic relationship and the presumed value of dreams as sources of insight into unconscious desires.

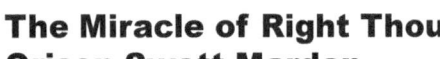

Dream Psychology
Psychoanalysis for Beginners

Sigmund Freud

Psychology   ISBN: *1-59462-905-6*

Pages:196

MSRP $15.45

The Miracle of Right Thought
Orison Swett Marden

QTY

Believe with all of your heart that you will do what you were made to do. When the mind has once formed the habit of holding cheerful, happy, prosperous pictures, it will not be easy to form the opposite habit. It does not matter how improbable or how far away this realization may see, or how dark the prospects may be, if we visualize them as best we can, as vividly as possible, hold tenaciously to them and vigorously struggle to attain them, they will gradually become actualized, realized in the life. But a desire, a longing without endeavor, a yearning abandoned or held indifferently will vanish without realization.

Pages:360

Self Help   ISBN: *1-59462-644-8*

MSRP $25.45

The Rosicrucian Cosmo-Conception Mystic Christianity by *Max Heindel*   ISBN: *1-59462-188-8*   **$38.95**
The Rosicrucian Cosmo-conception is not dogmatic, neither does it appeal to any other authority than the reason of the student. It is: not controversial, but is: sent forth in the, hope that it may help to clear...   New Age/Religion Pages 646

Abandonment To Divine Providence by *Jean-Pierre de Caussade*   ISBN: *1-59462-228-0*   **$25.95**
"The Rev. Jean Pierre de Caussade was one of the most remarkable spiritual writers of the Society of Jesus in France in the 18th Century. His death took place at Toulouse in 1751. His works have gone through many editions and have been republished...   Inspirational/Religion Pages 400

Mental Chemistry by *Charles Haanel*   ISBN: *1-59462-192-6*   **$23.95**
Mental Chemistry allows the change of material conditions by combining and appropriately utilizing the power of the mind. Much like applied chemistry creates something new and unique out of careful combinations of chemicals the mastery of mental chemistry...   New Age Pages 354

The Letters of Robert Browning and Elizabeth Barret Barrett 1845-1846 vol II   ISBN: *1-59462-193-4*   **$35.95**
by *Robert Browning and Elizabeth Barret*   Biographies Pages 596

Gleanings In Genesis (volume I) by *Arthur W. Pink*   ISBN: *1-59462-130-6*   **$27.45**
Appropriately has Genesis been termed "the seed plot of the Bible" for in it we have, in germ form, almost all of the great doctrines which are afterwards fully developed in the books of Scripture which follow...   Religion/Inspirational Pages 420

The Master Key by *L. W. de Laurence*   ISBN: *1-59462-001-6*   **$30.95**
In no branch of human knowledge has there been a more lively increase of the spirit of research during the past few years than in the study of Psychology, Concentration and Mental Discipline. The requests for authentic lessons in Thought Control, Mental Discipline and...   New Age/Business Pages 422

The Lesser Key Of Solomon Goetia by *L. W. de Laurence*   ISBN: *1-59462-092-X*   **$9.95**
This translation of the first book of the "Lernegton" which is now for the first time made accessible to students of Talismanic Magic was done, after careful collation and edition, from numerous Ancient Manuscripts in Hebrew, Latin, and French...   New Age/Occult Pages 92

Rubaiyat Of Omar Khayyam by *Edward Fitzgerald*   ISBN:*1-59462-332-5*   **$13.95**
Edward Fitzgerald, whom the world has already learned, in spite of his own efforts to remain within the shadow of anonymity, to look upon as one of the rarest poets of the century, was born at Bredfield, in Suffolk, on the 31st of March, 1809. He was the third son of John Purcell...   Music Pages 172

Ancient Law by *Henry Maine*   ISBN: *1-59462-128-4*   **$29.95**
The chief object of the following pages is to indicate some of the earliest ideas of mankind, as they are reflected in Ancient Law, and to point out the relation of those ideas to modern thought.   Religion/History Pages 452

Far-Away Stories by *William J. Locke*   ISBN: *1-59462-129-2*   **$19.45**
"Good wine needs no bush, but a collection of mixed vintages does. And this book is just such a collection. Some of the stories I do not want to remain buried for ever in the museum files of dead magazine-numbers an author's not unpardonable vanity..."   Fiction Pages 272

Life of David Crockett by *David Crockett*   ISBN: *1-59462-250-7*   **$27.45**
"Colonel David Crockett was one of the most remarkable men of the times in which he lived. Born in humble life, but gifted with a strong will, an indomitable courage, and unremitting perseverance...   Biographies/New Age Pages 424

Lip-Reading by *Edward Nitchie*   ISBN: *1-59462-206-X*   **$25.95**
Edward B. Nitchie, founder of the New York School for the Hard of Hearing, now the Nitchie School of Lip-Reading, Inc, wrote "LIP-READING Principles and Practice". The development and perfecting of this meritorious work on lip-reading was an undertaking...   How-to Pages 400

A Handbook of Suggestive Therapeutics, Applied Hypnotism, Psychic Science   ISBN: *1-59462-214-0*   **$24.95**
by *Henry Munro*   Health/New Age/Health/Self-help Pages 376

A Doll's House: and Two Other Plays by *Henrik Ibsen*   ISBN: *1-59462-112-8*   **$19.95**
Henrik Ibsen created this classic when in revolutionary 1848 Rome. Introducing some striking concepts in playwriting for the realist genre, this play has been studied the world over.   Fiction/Classics/Plays 308

The Light of Asia by *sir Edwin Arnold*   ISBN: *1-59462-204-3*   **$13.95**
In this poetic masterpiece, Edwin Arnold describes the life and teachings of Buddha. The man who was to become known as Buddha to the world was born as Prince Gautama of India but he rejected the worldly riches and abandoned the reigns of power when...   Religion/History/Biographies Pages 170

The Complete Works of Guy de Maupassant by *Guy de Maupassant*   ISBN: *1-59462-157-8*   **$16.95**
"For days and days, nights and nights, I had dreamed of that first kiss which was to consecrate our engagement, and I knew not on what spot I should put my lips..."   Fiction/Classics Pages 240

The Art of Cross-Examination by *Francis L. Wellman*   ISBN: *1-59462-309-0*   **$26.95**
Written by a renowned trial lawyer, Wellman imparts his experience and uses case studies to explain how to use psychology to extract desired information through questioning.   How-to/Science/Reference Pages 408

Answered or Unanswered? by *Louisa Vaughan*   ISBN: *1-59462-248-5*   **$10.95**
Miracles of Faith in China   Religion Pages 112

The Edinburgh Lectures on Mental Science (1909) by *Thomas*   ISBN: *1-59462-008-3*   **$11.95**
This book contains the substance of a course of lectures recently given by the writer in the Queen Street Hall, Edinburgh. Its purpose is to indicate the Natural Principles governing the relation between Mental Action and Material Conditions...   New Age/Psychology Pages 148

Ayesha by *H. Rider Haggard*   ISBN: *1-59462-301-5*   **$24.95**
Verily and indeed it is the unexpected that happens! Probably if there was one person upon the earth from whom the Editor of this, and of a certain previous history, did not expect to hear again...   Classics Pages 380

Ayala's Angel by *Anthony Trollope*   ISBN: *1-59462-352-X*   **$29.95**
The two girls were both pretty, but Lucy who was twenty-one who supposed to be simple and comparatively unattractive, whereas Ayala was credited, as her Bombwhat romantic name might show, with poetic charm and a taste for romance. Ayala when her father died was nineteen...   Fiction Pages 484

The American Commonwealth by *James Bryce*   ISBN: *1-59462-286-8*   **$34.45**
An interpretation of American democratic political theory. It examines political mechanics and society from the perspective of Scotsman James Bryce   Politics Pages 572

Stories of the Pilgrims by *Margaret P. Pumphrey*   ISBN: *1-59462-116-0*   **$17.95**
This book explores pilgrims religious oppression in England as well as their escape to Holland and eventual crossing to America on the Mayflower, and their early days in New England...   History Pages 268

QTY

The Fasting Cure *by Sinclair Upton*   ISBN: *1-59462-222-1* **$13.95**

In the Cosmopolitan Magazine for May, 1910, and in the Contemporary Review (London) for April, 1910, I published an article dealing with my experiences in fasting. I have written a great many magazine articles, but never one which attracted so much attention... New Age/Self Help/Health Pages 164

Hebrew Astrology *by Sepharial*   ISBN: *1-59462-308-2* **$13.45**

In these days of advanced thinking it is a matter of common observation that we have left many of the old landmarks behind and that we are now pressing forward to greater heights and to a wider horizon than that which represented the mind-content of our progenitors... Astrology Pages 144

Thought Vibration or The Law of Attraction in the Thought World   ISBN: *1-59462-127-6* **$12.95**

by William Walker Atkinson   Psychology/Religion Pages 144

Optimism *by Helen Keller*   ISBN: *1-59462-108-X* **$15.95**

Helen Keller was blind, deaf, and mute since 19 months old, yet famously learned how to overcome these handicaps, communicate with the world, and spread her lectures promoting optimism. An inspiring read for everyone... Biographies/Inspirational Pages 84

Sara Crewe *by Frances Burnett*   ISBN: *1-59462-360-0* **$9.45**

In the first place, Miss Minchin lived in London. Her home was a large, dull, tall one, in a large, dull square, where all the houses were alike, and all the sparrows were alike, and where all the door-knockers made the same heavy sound... Childrens/Classic Pages 88

The Autobiography of Benjamin Franklin *by Benjamin Franklin*   ISBN: *1-59462-135-7* **$24.95**

The Autobiography of Benjamin Franklin has probably been more extensively read than any other American historical work, and no other book of its kind has had such ups and downs of fortune. Franklin lived for many years in England, where he was agent... Biographies/History Pages 332

Name	
Email	
Telephone	
Address	
City, State ZIP	

☐ **Credit Card**   ☐ **Check / Money Order**

Credit Card Number	
Expiration Date	
Signature	

Please Mail to: Book Jungle
PO Box 2226
Champaign, IL 61825
or Fax to: 630-214-0564

ORDERING INFORMATION

web: *www.bookjungle.com*
email: *sales@bookjungle.com*
fax: *630-214-0564*
mail: *Book Jungle PO Box 2226 Champaign, IL 61825*
or PayPal *to sales@bookjungle.com*

Please contact us for bulk discounts

DIRECT-ORDER TERMS

**20% Discount if You Order
Two or More Books**
Free Domestic Shipping!
Accepted: Master Card, Visa,
Discover, American Express

www.ingramcontent.com/pod-product-compliance
Lightning Source LLC
Chambersburg PA
CBHW081201170626
46813CB00009B/3273